Dear Karyn,
Merry Christmas 2018!
Love,
Ty, Michelle, Avery & Elliot

Dear Karyn,
Merry Christmas 2018!

This book belongs to

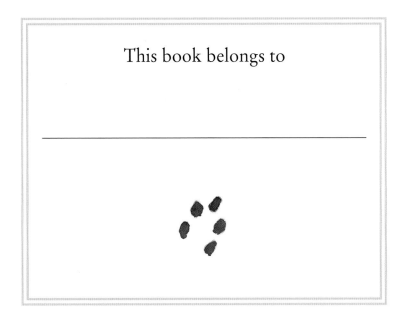

_____

HarperFestival is an imprint of HarperCollins Publishers.

Library of Congress catalog card number: 2013956797
ISBN 978-0-06-231242-6 (trade bdg.)

Typography by Rick Farley
18 19 SCP 10 9 8
❖
Originally published in hardcover in Great Britain by HarperCollins Children's Books in 2010
First US edition, 2014

Michael Bond

The PADDiNGTON Treasury

Six classic bedtime stories about the bear from Peru

illustrated by R. W. ALLEY

HARPER
An Imprint of HarperCollins Publishers

Contents

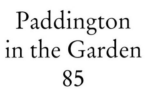

Introduction

One of the nice things about being a writer is that you are never entirely alone. Your characters go with you.

I count myself lucky in having Paddington as a traveling companion. Imagine how it would be if you had someone you didn't like looking over your shoulder all the time!

Paddington has an enquiring mind, and he often sees things in an entirely different light, so positions get reversed. I find myself tagging alongside him, wondering what would happen if he were wearing my shoes?

Sometimes he comes up with surprising answers, leaving me to find a way out of his predicament as best I can.

I hope you get as much pleasure out of reading the following six stories as I did writing them.

Michael Bond

Paddington

Mr. and Mrs. Brown first met Paddington on a railway platform. In fact, that was how he came to have such an unusual name for a bear, because Paddington was the name of the station.

The Browns were waiting to meet their daughter, Judy, when Mr. Brown noticed something small and furry near the LOST LUGGAGE office. "It looks like a bear," he said.

"A bear?" repeated Mrs. Brown. "In Paddington Station? Don't be silly, Henry. There can't be!"

But Mr. Brown was right. It was sitting on an old leather suitcase marked WANTED ON VOYAGE, and as they drew near it stood up and politely raised its hat.

"Good afternoon," it said. "May I help you?"

"It's very kind of you," said Mr. Brown, "but as a matter of fact, we were wondering if we could help *you*?"

"You're a very small bear," said Mrs. Brown. "Where are you from?"

The bear looked around carefully before replying.

"Darkest Peru. I'm not really supposed to be here at all. I'm a stowaway."

"You don't mean to say you've come all the way from
South America on your own?" exclaimed Mrs. Brown.
"Whatever did you do for food?"

Unlocking the suitcase, the bear took out an almost empty
glass jar. "I ate marmalade," it said. "Bears like marmalade."

Mrs. Brown looked at the label around the bear's neck. It said, quite simply,

PLEASE LOOK
AFTER THIS
BEAR. Thank
you.

"Oh, Henry!" she cried. "We can't leave him here all by himself. There's no knowing what might happen to him. Can't he come home and stay with us?"

"Stay with us?" repeated Mr. Brown nervously.

He looked down at the bear. "Er, would you like that?" he asked. "That is," he added hastily, "if you have nothing else planned."

"Oooh, yes," replied the bear. "I would like that very much. I've nowhere to go and everyone seems in such a hurry."

"That settles it," said Mrs. Brown. "Now, you must be thirsty after your journey. Mr. Brown can get you some tea while I go and meet our daughter, Judy."

"But, Mary," said Mr. Brown, "we don't even know its name."

Mrs. Brown thought for a moment. "I know," she said. "We'll call him Paddington—after the station."

"Paddington!" The bear tested it several times to make sure. "It sounds very important."

Mr. Brown tried it out next. "Follow me, Paddington," he said. "I'll take you to the snack bar."

Mr. Brown was as good as his word. Paddington had never seen so many snacks on one tray and he didn't know which to try first.

He was so hungry and thirsty he climbed up on the table to get a better look.

Mr. Brown turned away, pretending he had tea with a bear in Paddington Station every day of his life.

"Henry!" cried Mrs. Brown when she arrived with Judy. "What *are* you doing to that poor bear?"

Paddington jumped up to raise his hat, and in his haste, he stepped on a strawberry tart, skidded on the cream, and fell over backward into his cup of tea.

"I think we'd better go before anything else happens," said
Mr. Brown.

Judy took hold of Paddington's paw. "Come along," she
said. "We'll take you home and you can meet Mrs. Bird and
my brother, Jonathan."

Mr. Brown led the way to a waiting taxi. "Number thirty-two Windsor Gardens, please," he said.

The driver stared at Paddington. "Bears is extra," he growled. "Sticky bears is twice as much. And make sure none of it comes off on my interior. It was clean when I set out this morning."

The sun was shining as they drove out of the station, and there were cars and big red buses everywhere. Paddington waved to some people waiting at a bus stop, and several of them waved back. It was all very friendly.

Paddington tapped the taxi driver on his shoulder. "It isn't a bit like Darkest Peru," he announced.

The man jumped at the sound of Paddington's voice. "Cream!" he said bitterly. "Cream and jam all over me coat!" He slid the little window behind him shut.

"Oh dear, Henry," murmured Mrs. Brown. "I wonder if we're doing the right thing?"

Fortunately, before anyone had time to answer, they arrived at Windsor Gardens and Judy helped Paddington onto the pavement.

"Now you're going to meet Mrs. Bird," she said. "She looks after us. She's a bit fierce at times, but she doesn't really mean it. I'm sure you'll like her."

Paddington felt his knees begin to wobble. "I'm sure I shall, if you say so," he replied. "The thing is, will she like *me*?"

"Goodness gracious!" exclaimed Mrs. Bird. "What *have* you got there?"

"It's not a what," said Judy. "It's a bear called Paddington and he's coming to stay with us."

"A bear," said Mrs. Bird, as Paddington raised his hat. "Well, he has good manners, I'll say that for him."

"I'm afraid I stepped on a jam tart by mistake," said Paddington.

"I can see that," said Mrs. Bird. "You'd better have a bath before you're very much older. Judy can turn it on for you. I daresay you'll be wanting some marmalade, too!"

"I think she likes you," whispered Judy.

Paddington had never been in a
bathroom before, and while the
water was running he made
himself at home. First of all,
he tried writing his new
name in the steam on the
mirror.

Then he used Mr. Brown's shaving
foam to draw a map of Peru on the
floor. It wasn't until a drip
landed on his head that
he remembered what
he was supposed
to be doing.

He soon discovered that getting into a bath is one thing, but it's quite another matter getting out again—especially when it's full of soapy water.

Paddington
tried calling out,
"Help!"—at first
in a quiet voice so
as not to disturb
anyone, then very
loudly,

"HELP!

HELP!"

When that didn't
work, he began bailing
the water out with his
hat. But the hat had
several holes in it, and
his map of Peru soon
turned into a sea of
foam.

Suddenly, Jonathan and Judy burst into the bathroom and lifted a dripping Paddington onto the floor.

"Thank goodness you're all right!" cried Judy. "We heard you calling out."

"Fancy making such a mess," said Jonathan admiringly. "You should have pulled the plug out."

"Oh!" said Paddington. "I never thought of that."

When Paddington came downstairs, he looked so clean no one could possibly be cross with him. His fur was all soft and silky, his nose gleamed, and his paws had lost all traces of the jam and cream.

The Browns made room for him in a small armchair, and Mrs. Bird brought him a pot of tea and a plate of hot buttered toast and marmalade.

"Now," said Mrs. Brown, "you must tell us all about yourself. I'm sure you must have had lots of adventures."

"I have," said Paddington earnestly. "Things are always happening to me. I'm that sort of a bear." He settled back in the armchair.

"I was brought up by my aunt Lucy in Darkest Peru," he began. "But she had to go into the Home for Retired Bears in Lima." He closed his eyes thoughtfully and a hush fell over the room as everyone waited expectantly.

After a while, when nothing happened, they began to get restless. Mr. Brown tried coughing. Then he reached across and poked Paddington.

"Well I never," he said. "I do believe he's fast asleep!"

"After all that's happened to him," said Mrs. Brown, "is it any wonder?"

Paddington
at the Palace

One morning Paddington and Mr. Gruber set out to see the Changing of the Guard at Buckingham Palace.

Mr. Gruber took his camera, Paddington took a flag on a stick in case he saw the Queen, and they both sat on the front seat of the bus so that they could see all the places of interest on the way.

The bus took them most of the way, and then they had to
walk through St. James's Park.

It was a lovely sunny morning and there were flowers
everywhere.

"I think I may pick some for the Queen," said Paddington.

"I'm afraid that's against the law," said Mr. Gruber. "This is what is known as a Royal Park, and all the flowers belong to the Queen anyway. Besides, it would spoil it for others.

"If you like I'll take a picture for your scrapbook instead."

"Fancy having a front garden as big as this," said Paddington. "I wonder if she has to mow the lawn?"

Mr. Gruber laughed and then, as they drew near to some large gates, he pointed towards the roof of a building behind them.

"We're in luck's way, Mr. Brown," he said. "There's a flag flying. That means the Queen is at home."

Paddington peered through the railings and waved his own
flag several times in case the Queen was watching.

"I think I saw someone at one of the windows, Mr.
Gruber," he called excitedly. "Do you think it was the
Queen?"

"Who knows?" said Mr. Gruber.

Soon afterwards they heard the sound of a band playing. The music got louder and louder and there was a lot of shouting and the *clump, clump* of marching feet.

But by then there were so many people, Paddington
couldn't see a thing.

Mr. Gruber wondered whether he ought to suggest holding Paddington up to see, but in the end he bought him a periscope instead.

"If you look through the bottom end," he explained, "you can see over the tops of people's heads."

Paddington tried it out, but all he could see were other people's faces and he didn't think much of some of those.

In the end he tried crawling through the legs of the crowd, but by the time he got to the other side the band had passed by.

"Look," said a small boy, pointing at Paddington. "One of the soldiers has dropped his hat."

"It's what they call a busby, dear," said his mother.

Paddington jumped to his feet. "I'm not a *busby*," he cried. "I'm a bear!"

Gradually the crowd melted away until there were only a few people left.

"Oh dear," said Mr. Gruber. "It's all over and I didn't even get a picture of you with one of the guardsmen."

"I didn't even *see* them," said Paddington sadly.

Just then a man in a bowler hat said something to a policeman
by the gate, and then pointed towards Paddington and Mr. Gruber.

The policeman beckoned to them. "I've instructions to invite you inside so that you can take a proper photograph," he called. "You're very honored."

Paddington felt most important as he and Mr. Gruber followed the policeman across the palace parade ground and the guard came to attention.

"I think," he said, as he stood to attention while Mr. Gruber took a photograph, "this guard is so good he doesn't need changing."

As they left the palace, Paddington stopped by the gates to wave his flag.

"Do you think it was the Queen looking out of the window when we first came?" he asked.

"It was either the Queen," said Mr. Gruber, "or it was someone who likes bears very much."

And he took one last picture for Paddington's scrapbook. "You must mark the window with a cross when you paste it in—just in case."

Me at the palace.

Paddington
at the Zoo

One day Jonathan and Judy decided to take Paddington on an outing to the zoo.

Before they set off Paddington made a large pile of marmalade sandwiches—six in all.

But when they reached the zoo, the gatekeeper wouldn't let them in.

"I'm sorry," he said. "Pets aren't allowed."

"Pets!" repeated Jonathan.

"Paddington isn't a *pet*," said Judy. "He's one of the family."

And Paddington gave the man such a hard stare he let them in without another word.

"Come on," said Jonathan. "Why don't I take your picture with the parrot?"

"Give a great big smile," called Judy. "Say cheese!"

"Cheese," said Paddington.

"Squawk!" said a parrot as it took a big bite out of
Paddington's sandwich. "Thank you very much. Squawk!
Squawk!"

Next they went to see the Siberian Wild Dog.

"Nice doggie," said Paddington.

But the Siberian Wild Dog went, "Owwowwwowwwoo!" and made Paddington jump so much the rest of the sandwich flew out of his hand and landed in the cage.

"Let me take a picture of you with a donkey," said Jonathan.

"Hee! Haw!" brayed the donkey when it saw Paddington's sandwiches.

"That's two gone," said Judy.

Paddington's smile was getting less cheesy all the time.

The elephant didn't wait to be asked either.
It simply made a loud trumpeting noise—
"Whoooohoowooo!"—
and reached down
with its trunk.

Paddington watched as his third sandwich disappeared.
He began to feel that going to the zoo was not such a good
idea after all.

But there was worse to follow.

When the lion saw them coming, it gave a great roar—
"Grrrrrrrrahh!"

It was such a loud roar Paddington dropped his fourth sandwich on the ground, and before he could say help it was surrounded by pigeons.

The only ones who didn't
say anything were the
penguins. They just stood there
looking sad, as if they were all
dressed up for a party but had
nowhere to go.

Paddington felt so sorry for
them he gave them sandwich
number five.

"Penguins eat fish," said a
man sternly. He pointed to a
notice. "It is strictly forbidden
to give them marmalade
sandwiches."

And while Paddington was looking at the notice, the man helped himself to the last of the sandwiches!

"The cheek of it!" said Jonathan.

"You need eyes in the back of your head," agreed Judy.

"I need my elevenses," said Paddington. "Zoos make you hungry. Besides, nothing more can happen to me now."

But it did. Just to round things off, the mountain goat ate his sandwich bag!

"That does it!" said Jonathan. "If you ask me, it's time we went home."

A few days later Jonathan showed Paddington the photographs he'd taken at the zoo. "You can have one for your scrapbook," he said.

"Which do you like best?" asked Judy.

"The one with the parrot," said Paddington promptly. "At least he said thank you when he ate my marmalade sandwich. That's more than any of the others did!"

Paddington
in the Garden

One morning Paddington went out into the garden and began making a list of all the nice things he could think of about being a bear and living with the Browns.

He had a room of his own and a warm bed to sleep in. And he had marmalade for breakfast *every* morning. In Darkest Peru he had only been allowed to have it on Sundays.

The list was soon so long he had nearly run out of paper before he realized he had left out one of the nicest things of all…

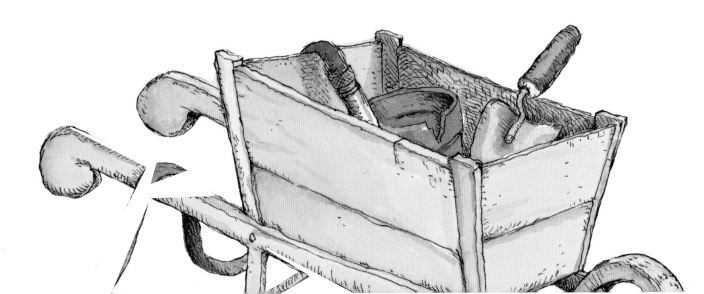

...the garden itself!

Paddington liked the Browns' garden. Apart from the occasional noise from a nearby building site, it was so quiet and peaceful it didn't seem like being in London at all.

But nice gardens don't just happen. They usually require a lot of hard work, and the one at number thirty-two Windsor Gardens was no exception. Mr. Brown had to mow the lawn twice a week, and Mrs. Brown was kept busy weeding the flower beds. There was always something to do. Even Mrs. Bird lent a hand whenever she had a spare moment.

It was Mrs. Bird who first suggested giving Jonathan, Judy, and Paddington each a piece of the garden.

"It will keep certain bears out of mischief," she said meaningly. "And it will be fun for Jonathan and Judy as well."

Mr. Brown agreed it was a very good idea, and he marked out three plots at the far end of the lawn.

Paddington was most excited. "I don't suppose there are many bears who have their own garden!" he exclaimed.

Early the next morning all three set to work.

Judy decided to make a flower bed and Jonathan had his eye on some old paving stones.

Paddington didn't know what to do. In the past he had often found that gardening was much harder than it looked, especially when you only had paws.

In the end, armed with a jar of Mrs. Bird's homemade marmalade, he borrowed Mr. Brown's wheelbarrow and set off to look for ideas.

His first stop was a stall in the market, where he bought a book called *How to Plan Your Garden* by Lionel Trug.

It came complete with a large packet of assorted seeds, and if the picture on the front cover was anything to go by, it was no wonder Mr. Trug looked happy, for he seemed to do most of his planning while lying in a hammock. By the end of the book, without lifting a finger, he was surrounded by blooms.

Paddington decided it was a very good value indeed—especially when the owner of the stall gave him two pence change.

Mr. Trug's book was full of useful hints and tips.

The first one suggested that before starting work it was a good idea to close your eyes and try to picture what the garden would look like when it was finished.

Having walked into a lamppost by mistake, Paddington decided to read another page or two, and there he found a much better idea. Mr. Trug advised standing back and looking at the site from a safe distance, preferably somewhere high up.

Paddington knew just the spot.

By the time Paddington reached the
building site near the Browns' house it
was the middle of the morning, and the
men were all on their tea break.

Placing his jar of marmalade on a
wooden platform for safekeeping, he
sat on a pile of bricks for a rest while he
considered the matter.

There was no one about....

And there was a ladder nearby....

Mr. Trug was quite right. The Browns'
garden did look very different from
high up. But before he had time to get
his breath back, Paddington heard the
sound of an engine starting up. He peered
through a gap in the boards. As he did so
his eyes nearly popped out.

On the ground just below him, a man
was emptying a load of concrete on the very spot where he
had left his jar of marmalade!

Paddington scrambled back down the ladder as fast as
his legs would carry him, reaching the bottom just as the
foreman came around a corner.

"Is anything wrong?" asked the man. "You look upset."

"My jar's been buried!" exclaimed Paddington hotly, pointing to the pile of concrete. "It had some of Mrs. Bird's best golden chunks in it, too!"

"I won't ask how your jar got there," said the foreman, turning to Paddington as his men set to work clearing the concrete into small piles, "*or* what you were doing up the ladder."

"I'm glad of that," said Paddington, politely raising his hat.

Suddenly there was a whirring
sound from somewhere overhead, and
to Paddington's surprise the platform
landed at his feet. "My marmalade!"
he exclaimed thankfully.

"Your *marmalade*?" repeated the foreman, staring at the jar. "Did you say marmalade?"

"That's right," said Paddington. "I put it there ready for my elevenses. It must have been taken up by mistake. Now the top's come off!"

It was the foreman's turn to look as though he could hardly believe his eyes.

"That's special quick-drying cement!" he wailed. "It's probably rock-hard already—ruined by a bear's marmalade! No one will give me tuppence for it now!"

"I will," said Paddington eagerly. "I've had an idea!"

Paddington was busy for the rest of the week.

When the builders saw the rock garden he had made, they were most impressed, and the foreman even gave him some plants to finish it off until his seeds started to grow.

"It's National Garden Day on Saturday," he said. "There are some very famous people judging it. I'll spread the word around. You never know your luck."

The foreman was as good as his word, and on Saturday half the neighborhood turned up at number thirty-two Windsor Gardens to see the judges arrive.

Paddington nearly fell over backwards with surprise when he discovered that no less a person than Mr. Lionel Trug himself was leading the procession.

"It's very good of you to get out of your hammock, Mr. Trug!" he exclaimed.

"Er…not at all," said Lionel Trug. "My pleasure. I must say, I love your orange stones. Where *did* you find them?"

"I didn't," said Paddington. "I think they found me. Thanks to the builders."

"Congratulations!" said Mr. Trug, as he handed Paddington a gold star. "It's good to see a young bear taking up gardening. I hope you will be the first of many."

"Who would have believed it?" said Mr. Brown, as the last of the crowd departed.

"You must write and tell Aunt Lucy all about it," said Mrs. Bird. "They'll be very excited in the Home for Retired Bears when they hear the news."

Paddington thought that was a good idea, but he had something to do first.

He wanted to add one more important item to his list of all
the nice things there were about being a bear and living with
the Browns:

HAVING MY OWN ROCK GARDEN!

Then he signed his name and
added his special paw print…
just to show it was genuine.

Dear Aunt Lucy,

Aunt Lucy
Home for Retired
Bears,
Lima, Peru

Paddington
and the
Marmalade Maze

One day, Paddington's friend Mr. Gruber took him on an outing to a place called Hampton Court Palace.

"I think you will enjoy it, Mr. Brown," he said as they drew near. "It's very old and it has over one thousand rooms. Lots of kings and queens have lived here."

Paddington always enjoyed his outings with Mr. Gruber, and he couldn't wait to see inside the palace.

As they made their way through an arch, Mr. Gruber pointed to a large clock.

"That's a very special clock," he said. "It not only shows the time, it tells you what month it is."

"Perhaps we should hurry, Mr. Gruber," said Paddington anxiously. "It's half past June already."

They hadn't been inside the palace very long before they came across a room that had the biggest bed Paddington had ever seen.

"Queen Anne used to sleep in it," said Mr. Gruber.

"I expect they put the rope around it to stop her falling out when she had visitors," said Paddington, looking at all the people.

"This is known as the Haunted Gallery," said Mr. Gruber. "They do say that when Catherine Howard's ghost passes by you can feel a cold draft."

Paddington shivered. "I hope she's got a duffle coat like mine!" he said.

Mr. Gruber took Paddington to see the kitchen next.

"In the old days they used wood fires," he explained. "That's why there is such a high ceiling. There was a lot of smoke."

"I was hoping they might have left some royal buns behind," said Paddington, licking his lips.

"Speaking of buns," said Mr. Gruber, "I think it's time we had our lunch."

He led the way outside and they sat down together on the edge of a pool.

As Paddington opened his suitcase he accidentally dropped one of his sandwiches into the water. It was soon alive with goldfish.

"They must like marmalade," said Mr. Gruber. "I wonder if that's how they got their name?"

When they had finished their sandwiches, Mr. Gruber took Paddington to see The Great Vine.

"It's very famous," he said. "Every year they pick over five hundred bunches of grapes. Imagine that, Mr. Brown!"

"I'm trying to, Mr. Gruber," said Paddington. "I think I might plant a grape seed when I get back home."

Mr. Gruber chuckled. "I'm afraid you will have a long wait, Mr. Brown," he said. "That vine is over two hundred years old."

"Now," said Mr. Gruber, "before we leave we must visit the famous maze. Sometimes it takes people hours to find their way out."

"I hope that doesn't happen to us," said Paddington. "My paws are getting tired."

"Perhaps it's time I took you home," said Mr. Gruber.

Much to his surprise, the words were no sooner out of his mouth than everyone around them began to talk.

"Hey, that sounds like a great idea," said a man in a striped shirt.

"Please wait while I buy new film for my camera," said a lady in a purple shirt.

"I've never been inside a real English home before," said another lady. "I wonder if they serve tea?"

"Oh, dear!" whispered Mr. Gruber. "They must think I'm one of the guides. What shall we do?"

"Mrs. Bird won't be very pleased if they all follow us home," exclaimed Paddington. "She only has a small teapot."

Then he had an idea.

"Follow me," he called. "I think perhaps we ought to go in the maze after all."

"Are you sure we are doing the right thing?" said Mr. Gruber as he hurried on behind.

"Bears are good at mazes," said Paddington. "You need to be in Darkest Peru. The forests are very thick." And sure enough, before Mr. Gruber had time to say any more, Paddington led the way out, leaving everyone else inside.

"How ever did you manage to do that, Mr. Brown?" Mr. Gruber gasped.

"Quickest visit I've ever seen," agreed the man in the ticket office.

"I used marmalade chunks to show where we had been," said Paddington. "It's something my Aunt Lucy taught me before she went into the Home for Retired Bears."

"But I thought you had eaten all your sandwiches," said Mr. Gruber.

"I always keep a spare one under my hat in case I have an emergency," said Paddington. "That's something else Aunt Lucy taught me. She'll be very pleased when she hears."

And he stopped at a kiosk to buy a picture postcard so that he could write and tell her all about his day out.

That night when he went to bed, as well as the postcard and a pen, Paddington took some rope.

"It's something Queen Anne used to do," he announced. "I've a lot to tell Aunt Lucy and I don't want to fall out of bed before I've finished."

Paddington
the Artist

One Sunday Paddington was out for a walk with his friend Mr. Gruber when they came across some paintings tied to the railings outside the park.

"It's what is known as an outdoor exhibition," said Mr. Gruber. "They have one here every week when the weather is nice."

"All the paintings are for sale," Mr. Gruber explained. "This one is called *Sunset in Bombay*."

"I'm glad I don't live in Bombay," said Paddington. "It might keep me awake all night."

"How about this one then?" said Mr. Gruber. "It's called *Storm at Sea*."

Paddington suddenly wished he hadn't eaten such a big breakfast.

"I feel sick," he said, and he hurried on to the next picture.

"This is a picture the artist painted of himself," said Mr. Gruber. "It's called a self-portrait. I think it looks very much like him."

Paddington gave the picture a hard stare.

"I don't think I'll buy any paintings today, Mr. Gruber," he said.

Paddington looked very thoughtful as he made his way back home to number thirty-two Windsor Gardens.

When he got there, Paddington collected all his paints and brushes from his room and went out into the garden.

The next Sunday, when he and Mr. Gruber had finished their walk, Paddington led the way back towards Windsor Gardens.

"I'm having an outdoor exhibition of my own this week, Mr. Gruber," he said.

"This is meant to be a sunset in Windsor Gardens. Only it took me quite a long time and it got dark before I could finish it.

"And this is a picture of a rainstorm, only it got very wet and all the paint ran."

"This is my best one," said Paddington. "It's a picture of me. I've put my special paw mark on to show I painted it myself."

Mr. Gruber gazed at Paddington's portrait for a long time.

"It is very good, Mr. Brown," he said at last, not wishing to upset his friend, "but I think you look even better in real life."

"I kept going upstairs to look at myself in the mirror," said Paddington, "but by the time I got downstairs again I'd forgotten what I looked like."

"Painting isn't as easy as it looks," Paddington added
sadly, "especially with paws. I think I might give up."

"I hope you don't do that, Mr. Brown," Mr. Gruber said
thoughtfully.

After Mr. Gruber had said good-bye, Paddington sat down beside his paintings hoping that someone would stop and buy one.

But it was a warm day and no one came past. In the end Paddington fell asleep.

Paintings
for sale –
please pay
bear

When he woke up, Paddington found to his surprise that all his pictures had gone.

But tucked inside his duffle coat he found an envelope with his name on it: Mr. Paddington Brown, 32 Windsor Gardens. And inside the envelope there was some money and a note saying "Thank you."

If Mr. and Mrs. Brown recognized Mr. Gruber's writing they didn't say anything. They hadn't had such a peaceful time for ages.

And best of all, Paddington carried on painting. So everyone was happy.

"I think I may paint a family portrait now," said Paddington. "That is, if I have enough paint left for all the smiles."